To Jago – A. & C. Guillain

Farshore

First published in Great Britain 2021 by Farshore
An imprint of HarperCollinsPublishers
1 London Bridge Street, London SE1 9GF
www.farshorebooks.com

HarperCollinsPublishers
1st Floor, Watermarque Building, Ringsend Road
Dublin 4, Ireland

ISBN 978 1 4052 9626 7
Printed in China.
1

A CIP catalogue record for this title is available from the British Library.

Farshore takes its responsibility to the planet and its inhabitants very seriously.
We aim to use papers from well-managed forests run by responsible suppliers.

ONE POTATO TWO POTATOES

Adam & Charlotte Guillain

Sam Lloyd

Farshore

One potato,

two potatoes,

three
potatoes,
four . . .
Playing hide-and-seek, hang on –
who's that inside the drawer?

Five
potatoes,
six
potatoes,

seven potatoes . . . more!

Eight potatoes hear . . .

but can't quite reach the door.

Eight potatoes
in a tower
start to
tip and fall . . .

They crash out
through the door

and land in one potato ball!

"Your letter!" calls a lettuce

as they start to roll away.

"It has your invitation for the talent show today!"

Eight potatoes roll
for half an hour
down the street.

Oh no!

**They bowl a row of runner beans
right off their feet!**

Eight
potatoes roll downhill,
towards the talent show.

They find their invitation
and they line up in a row.

But eight potatoes can't be seen – they're too close to the floor!

So on their tiptoes eight potatoes sneak inside the door!

"We're prima ballerinas!"
calls a carrot, bowing low.
"Come and put a tutu on
so you can join our show!"

Eight potatoes put on tutus.
Whoops! They all fall down.

"These tutus are too big!"

cries one potato,
with a frown.

"Ha ha!"
laugh all the carrots
and make eight potatoes
sigh.
"We're much too small to dance," they say,
"so what else can we try?"

Eight potatoes spot some brave **spring onions** wearing hats.

One potato cries,
"Perhaps we could be acrobats?"

Caution: Practice session in full swing.

"Wow!"
gasp **eight** potatoes.

"Can we swing on your trapeze?"

Spring onions snort,
"You're far too short.
You barely reach our knees!"

Eight potatoes, shorter than a small spring onion's knees, spot a sporty **pineapple,** who's shooting hoops with ease.

"Let's try that!"

calls one potato, running for the ball.

"Potatoes?"
scoffs the pineapple.
"You're clearly
much too small!"

Eight potatoes at the biggest talent show in town,

watch a **beetroot** play the flute
while standing **upside down!**

One potato wails,
"It's our turn now!"

The rest gasp,
"Yikes!"

But then two new
potatoes come . . .

with shiny motorbikes!

"Their arms won't reach the handlebars!"
a row of **rhubarb** sneers.

A **turnip** laughs and calls,
"You're **much too** small **to change the gears!**"

When **ten potatoes** disappear . . .

the crowd begins to **boo.**

"They simply have no talent,"
laughs a cauliflower.
"No clue!"

But then the roar of engines makes the crowd let out a cheer.

And **WOW!** Ten proud potatoes . . .

in a pyramid
appear!
Ten potatoes shout,
"Ta-da!
We know that we are small.

But when
we stand together,
we're as gifted as you all!"